PRIMROSE, ARTHUR

and the

SECRET SOLUTION

MALCOLM KING

To order additional copies of this book, contact:

Xlibris
0800-056-3182
www.xlibrispublishing.co.uk
Orders@ Xlibrispublishing.co.uk

ISBN: Softcover   978-1-9845-9085-5
         EBook   978-1-9845-9086-2

Print information available on the last page

Rev. date: 08/08/2019

Primrose, Arthur and the Secret Solution

By Malcolm King

A picture book (for five year olds)

Summer had arrived.

Primrose (a song thrush) said to her younger
sister Debby and younger brother

Tim, "it's time for breakfast."

Swiftly they all flew to the ground.

The family were busy eating

Suddenly they heard, rustling in the bushes...

Then – "YEEEEEEK!"

Arthur (a young guinea pig) was frustrated.

He'd searched everywhere for heathy
food – but hadn't found any!

Emerging from behind a bush, "Hello," he said.

"Hi" Primrose said "we live up there," pointing to a tree.

"Then we are neighbours," said the
guinea pig. "As I live close by."

Rain started to bounce off the trees.

Debby cried "EEK!"

Arthur offered shelter.

Shelter in his home!

"You're a cool home!" said Tim.

"Um" agreed the others.

Primrose asked Arthur about himself.

He replied, "I'm lonely and wish I could find healthy food."

Primrose responded "I CAN MAKE YOUR WISHES COME TRUE" she said with a smile.

Arthur said "How about you?" She replied "I wish for help keeping my siblings safe whilst I get the families food."

Arthur responded "I CAN MAKE YOUR WISHES COME TRUE!" Arthur returned the smile.

So they made a plan.

The following day...

Arthur had organized a mini Sports Day.

First event was juggling. Debby won.

Second event was headstanding. Tim won.

Final event was the twenty five metres
running race. Arthur won.

Primrose asked, "Was it fun?"

"awesome time!" they said "We like Arthur."

Later that day Arthur heard "THUMP!" on his front door! Looking outside, he found a parcel!

That night...

Next day

Arthur invited Debby and Tim to see his tunnels.

"I want to show something you haven't seen before!"

They cautiously followed Arthur.

And further...

"Enjoy it?" Primrose asked.

"Epic!" cried Tim.

"Dark but interesting!" said Debby.

The following day

Primrose told Arthur "we want to show
something you have not seen before."

"Make yourself comfortable on my back, hold tight."

Soon they were flying high in the sky!

They flew over fields and houses. Excited Arthur felt the warm sun on his back.

And on...

Until...

A big wood pigeon was flying straight towards Primrose!

She swerved to avoid a collision – but straight into a pair of knickers on the washing line below! Arthur fell into a fast flowing river – with a loud SPLOSH!

Arthur was swept along, frantically reaching for overhanging branches. But one he managed to grab – snapped off. He tried again, it was stronger, but he went under water, losing his grip. Arthur resurfaced and stretched to reach...Tim grabbed his arms, saving him!

After a lunch break...

Flight continued...

They arrived at the allotment.

The children gather around them.

Suddenly, the birds heard a familiar song!

Deedle-dee, deedle-dee, deedle dee

Chip, chip, chip!

They knew it was mum singing!

The family were overjoyed!

Mum later told them she had been caught in a storm,
blown off course, damaged her wing-not been
able to fly back – but had since recovered!

Thanks to the kind children who looked after her.

They were told that they are always welcome
because the eat the crop pests.

And there is always food for Arthur!

So they agreed to visit every Tuesday.

After tea, it was time to fly home to
sleep and have happy dreams!

This is to thank all those people who have helped and supported me in the production of this book.

Including:-

Erica & Charles

Andrew & Iwona

Pen & Corrine

Lucy & Baz

Anne & Victor

Jill & Pat

Kay & Andy

Penny & Nicola

Printed in the United States
By Bookmasters